To Mark, Jess, Joe, and James

– J. H.

For Clarice Mary Alice and Vera Maud

– C. P.

tiger tales

5 River Road, Suite 128, Wilton, CT 06897

Published in the United States 2014

Originally published in Great Britain 2014

by Little Tiger Press

Text copyright © 2014 Julia Hubery

Illustrations copyright © 2014 Caroline Pedler

ISBN-13: 978-1-58925-164-9

ISBN-10: 1-58925-164-4

Printed in China

LTP/1400/0899/0314

For more insight and activities,
visit us at www.tigertalesbooks.com

When Grandma Saved Christmas

by Julia Hubery * Illustrated by Caroline Pedler

tiger tales

"Yippeeee! It's almost Christmas!" sang Bubble.
"And we're going to Grandma's!" added Squeak
as he helped Mommy pack his snowflake pajamas.
"Hurry up," smiled Mommy. "It's a long drive!"
"I wish we could fly to Grandma's," sighed Bubble,
"like Santa in his sleigh."

"Oh, no, Bubble!" cried Squeak. "How will Santa know we're at Grandma's? He might come here!"

"That's easy!" said Bubble. "We'll tell him!"

"We'll scooter to the North Pole,

pogo over the penguins, and hitch a polar-bear ride to Santa's workshop!"

"Wow! Do we have time for all of that?" asked Mommy. "How about writing Santa a letter?"

"We can do that, Mommy!" said Squeak
as they got to work. "Let's make it really BIG!"
"So Santa sees it!" agreed Bubble.

With snowy sparkles and glittery glue, they made the most wonderful letter ever.

"I wrote Santa's address in large letters to make sure!" Bubble told Squeak as Daddy helped them mail the letter.

But just as it dropped through the slot, Squeak cried, "Bubble! We forgot to tell Santa what Grandma's address is! How will he know where to go?"

"I know!" said Bubble.

"We'll bake a bazillion cookies . . .

and leave a trail for Rudolph to follow!"

"Sounds yummy!" said Daddy,
as they zoomed home.
"But Grandma's waiting
to see us. Could we
just leave Santa
a map?"

"We can do that, Daddy!" said Squeak.

Daddy helped Bubble
and Squeak draw a map,

and tape it to the door.

Then they helped Mommy
pack up the car.

"Hooray! We're off to Grandma's!"
everyone cheered as Mommy shut
the trunk.

On the way, they counted Christmas trees.

"I've seen two! Six! Twenty!" yelled Bubble.

"I've seen eighty-numpty-nine!" cried Squeak.

"That's not a number!" Bubble giggled.

"It is, IT IS—isn't it, Daddy?" shouted Squeak.

"Are we there yet?" sighed Daddy.

At last they saw Grandma's house,
sparkling in the snow.

"Grandma!" yelled Bubble and Squeak,
jumping into Grandma's arms.

"My favorite little mice!" she beamed.

Then, Bubble suddenly stopped.

"OH, NO!" he gasped, staring at Grandma's roof.

"Grandma, where's your chimney?"
cried Bubble.

"There isn't one!" squeaked Squeak.
"How will Santa get in?"
they both wailed.

"Don't worry," smiled Grandma.
"I've been very busy while I was
waiting for you. "

Bubble and Squeak followed Grandma
into her backyard.

"What's THAT!" they gasped.

"It's my Super-Swishy-Santa-Slide!"
said Grandma.

"Wow, Grandma!" cheered Squeak.

"Santa's sure to find us now!"
cried Bubble.

THIS WAY, SANTA!

The little mice swooped
and swished down the slide
until the stars began to twinkle,
and Grandma called, "Time for
hot chocolate!"

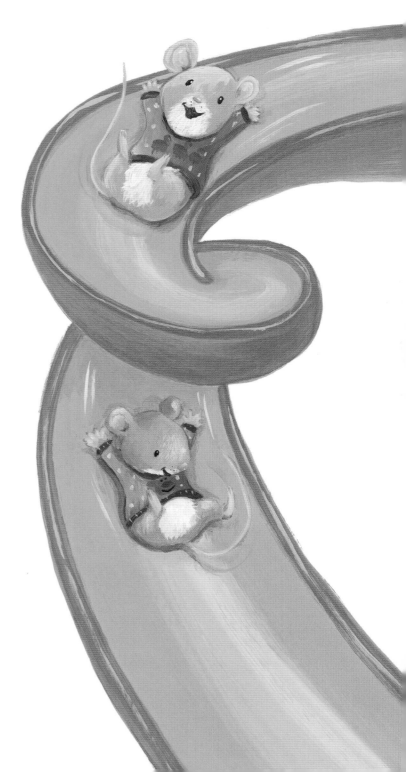

After hot chocolate and kisses, they wriggled into their pajamas, and Grandma read them a bedtime story.

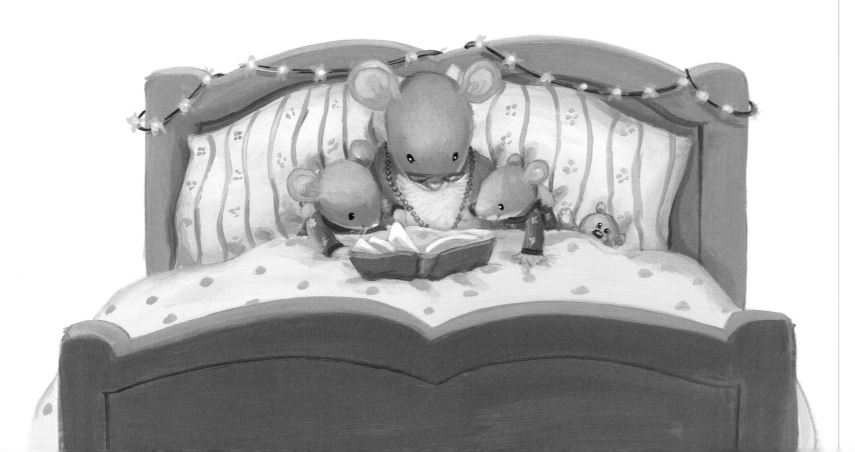

"Thanks for making sure Santa
finds us, Bubble," yawned Squeak
as the pair snuggled down to sleep.
"I hope he brings you lots of
presents."

And guess what?

Santa did!